KIT

The Incredible Litter Picker Kitter

EMMA LEASLEY

Illustrations by Ahmad Kardi

Kit is a cat that is mostly all black
With furry white socks
And tip of his tail.
He loves to cuddle
And to eat
He will happily greet you
With a purr
And a warbling wail.

Now Kit maybe that
A little clumsy, laid back,
But I assure you he is no ordinary kitter.

At sunset his vocation
Without any hesitation
Is gathering rubbish
And piles of old litter.

He boldly adventures
Up path's, Along fences,
in gardens, through woodland,
on streets.

Fetching home packets,
Discarded old rackets.
Chocolate wrappers
And half eaten treat's.

His hedgehog friend Sid
Got stuck in a lid
as he foraged and rifled.
He scurried away
Never returned to play
Because of a cup
that should have been recycled.

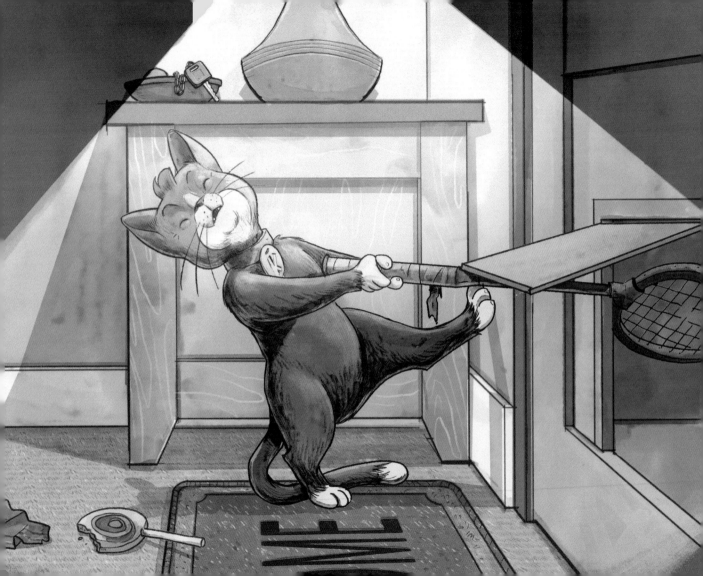

Kit's mission right then,
Was to never again,
Ignore the litter on the floor.
Whilst his human was sleeping
He went a creeping
Dragging junk through
his little kitty door.

Once hauled through the flap
Was a soggy old hat
Entangled with wool
And revolting rotten cuisine.

It didn't take long
For his human to locate the pong
That was formerly
A tin of sardines.
YUK

The bright eyes of the night
Watched on in great delight
As Kit the litter picking cat
In all his merriment
Cleaned up the environment
Giving his friends a safer habitat

Whilst out helping the planet
He disturbed grumpy old Janet,
The tabby from down number 10.
He realised his mistake
When he was met at the gate
With a hiss
Then chased back off again.

Through the daytime he slept,
Conserving energy for his quest
Of helping wildlife and saving the planet.
Dreaming of trash
And avoiding a clash
With his arch enemy
The tabby named Janet.

He couldn't be jollier
Our brave eco warrior
And although he is a curious kitter
Where there is rubbish and wrappers
And a world that matters
There will always be
Kit the litter picker kitter'.

The real life Kit

Printed in Great Britain
by Amazon